SANTA'S KEYS
STORY AND ILLUSTRATIONS
BY
SCOTT C. DURKIN

FOR ISADORA, AIDAN, PHENA AND HELEN

Published by SHAD PUBLISHING, London
Copyright © SHAD Publishing 2015
All rights reserved
ISBN: 978-0-9571238-2-3
http://www.santaskeys.com

"But I heard him exclaim, 'ere he drove out of sight, 'Happy Christmas to all, and to all a good-night!'"

Daddy closed the book.

"And I too say goodnight, my little angels. Sweet dreams. Sleep fast. Santa comes tonight!"

Daddy kissed Isadora, Aidan and the Baby goodnight.

He turned the lights out and closed the door.

"Isadora?"
whispered Aidan in the dark,

"Are you asleep?"

He waited
anxiously for
an answer.

"Dora?"

"Go to sleep,"

answered Isadora.

"We don't have a chimney,"
he declared.

The dark room
remained still.

"Dora! WE don't have a chimney!"

"No chimney,
no fireplace; no fireplace,
no Santa!"

"You have visited a lot of friends' houses for play dates. Do any of them have a chimney or fireplace?" she asked.

She stayed quiet for a moment. Despite the dark, she could see that her brother was thinking.

Isadora threw off her covers.

She found a jumper at the foot of her bed.

"Tell me, is it
cold outside?"
she asked.

"In our house, a machine in the basement called a 'furnace' heats up water and sends it all through the house. The hot water travels through pipes to radiators that fill each room with warmth."

"Not every family lives in a house like us.

Some people live in flats or apartments, others live in town houses or brownstones.

Some people even live in tents, mobile homes and on boats.

There are all kinds of homes.

Many of these homes do not have chimneys, and most are warmed by furnaces."

"As time passed, furnaces got smaller and burned hotter."

"Chimneys narrowed to such a degree that Santa just couldn't fit."

"What did Father Christmas do?" Aidan asked excitedly.

"Santa Claus is a wise
and experienced man."
said Isadora.
"So he applied all of
his experience and
wisdom to devise
an ingenious
solution.

He used
the door."

"Not very many people would lock their doors back then.

Santa could quietly slip inside, deliver his packages and...

...slip away without even a single smokey footprint."

"Now this worked for quite sometime, but the world was changing.

Cities bulged,

towns swelled...

and people began to lock their doors."

"It was at this point that Santa had to learn a new skill;

Locksmithing."

"A sturdy wooden desk was set in a small corner of Santa's North Pole workshop. The desk was followed by a pedal grinder, a weathered set of files, two clamps and a tin lantern."

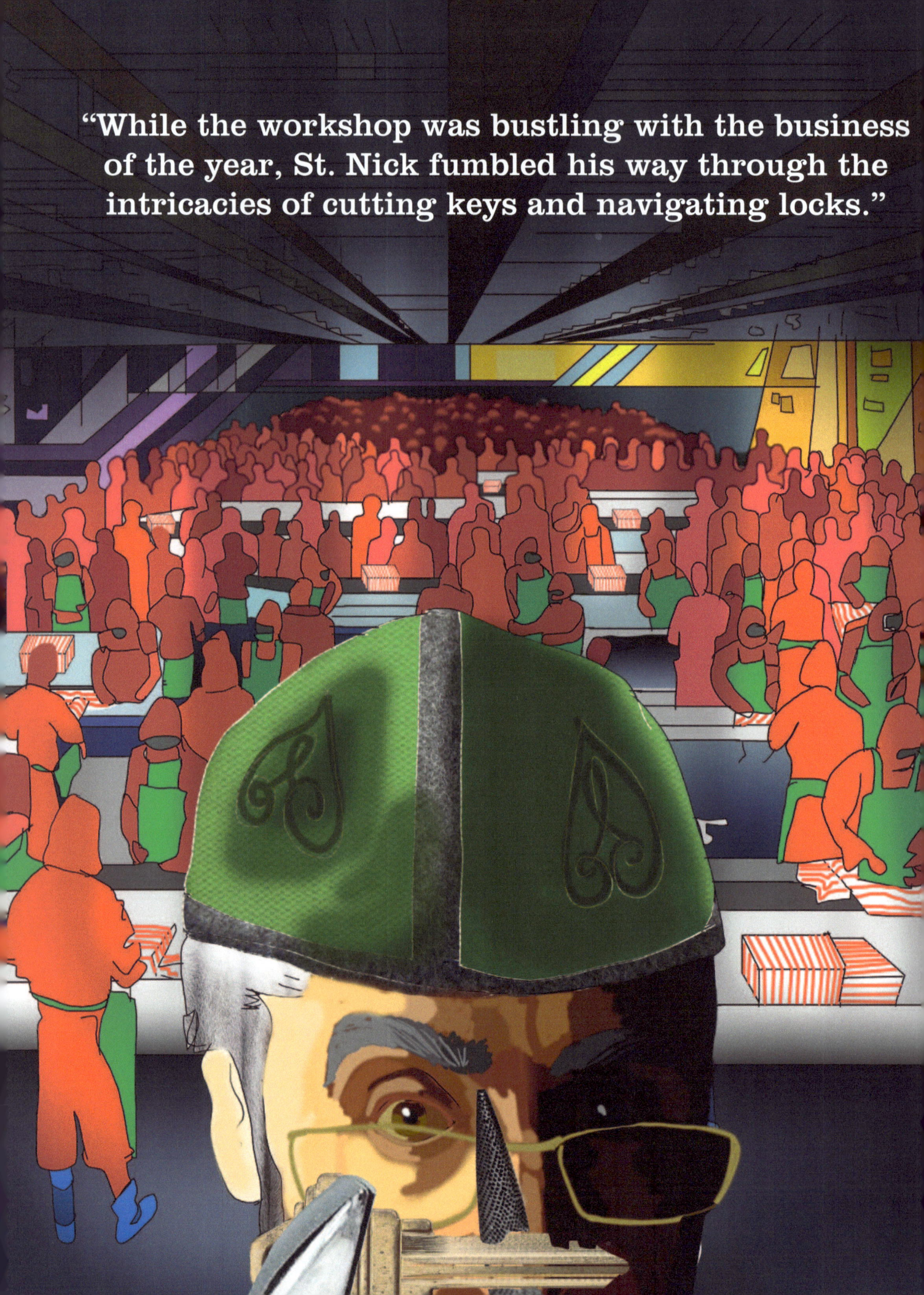

"While the workshop was bustling with the business of the year, St. Nick fumbled his way through the intricacies of cutting keys and navigating locks."

"During the first couple of years,
Santa got away with about a half-dozen keys."

"As the years passed, the keys multiplied. His keyring widened until thousands of keys made of every metal, in all shapes and sizes, jingled at his side."

"He will scan the lock and instinctively find our special key on his ring.

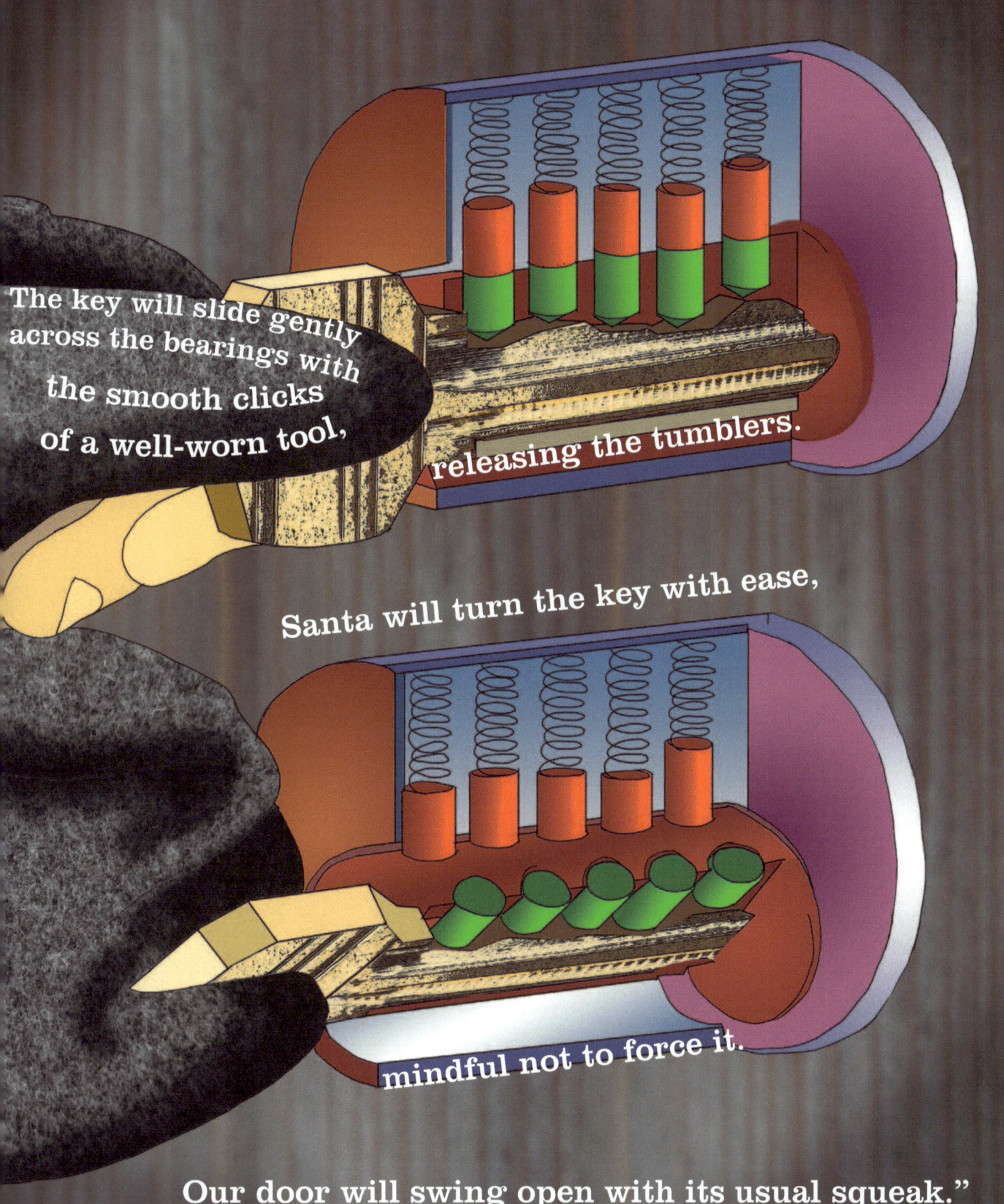

The key will slide gently across the bearings with the smooth clicks of a well-worn tool, releasing the tumblers.

Santa will turn the key with ease, mindful not to force it.

Our door will swing open with its usual squeak."

"The stockings will be filled,

the packages laid.

Cookies devoured and milk gulped down.

Santa will perhaps give the dogs a scratch.

He will pull the door shut behind him with a squeak. He will be gone.

www.ingramcontent.com/pod-product-compliance
Lightning Source LLC
Chambersburg PA
CBHW041004170626

46815CB00002B/150

9780957123823